A Weed Is a Seed

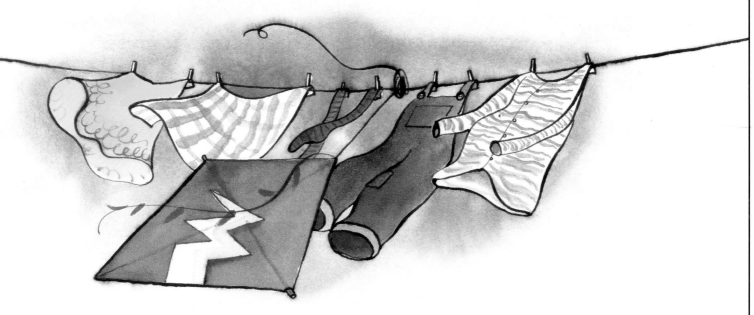

written by

FERIDA WOLFF

illustrated by

JANET PEDERSEN

Houghton Mifflin Company ⟩ *Boston New York 1996*

For information about this and other Houghton Mifflin
trade and reference books and multimedia products, visit
The Bookstore at Houghton Mifflin on the World Wide Web
at http://www.hmco.com/trade/.

Manufactured in the United States of America

Book design by David Saylor
The text of this book is set in 16-point Matt Antique.
The illustrations are watercolor and ink, reproduced in full color.

HOR 10 9 8 7 6 5 4 3 2 1

LIBRARY OF CONGRESS CATALOGING-IN-PUBLICATION DATA
Wolff, Ferida.
A weed is a seed / by Ferida Wolff ; illustrated by Janet Pedersen.
p.   cm.
Summary: Pairs of rhyming verses show that such things
in the natural world as weeds, a breeze, sand, and ice can
be seen both positively and negatively.
ISBN 0-395-72291-8
[1. Nature—Fiction. 2. Perspective (Philosophy)—Fiction.
3. Stories in rhyme.] I. Pedersen, Janet, ill. II. Title.
PZ8.3.W844We   1996
[E]—dc20   94-45505   CIP   AC

For Ronnie, the best sister in the whole world

F. W.

For Tom

J. P.

A weed is a seed
that just doesn't belong
in the place where it happens to grow.

But a weed can be feed
for a cold country mouse
digging out of the wintery snow.

A nest is a pest
when it's built on the roof
so it clogs up the drainpipe with leaves.

But a nest is the best
place to lay new white eggs
for a chicken that roosts in the eaves.

A kite is a sight,
blown off course by the wind,
with its tail tangled up in the vines.

But a kite taking flight
in the warm rising air
is a treat to see, over the pines.

A moth in the cloth
makes a hole in the sleeve
and a job for a needle and thread.

But a moth flying forth
from each flowering bud
helps the pollen of flowers to spread.

A breeze brings a sneeze
to a sensitive nose
that gets itches from roses and hay.

But a breeze in the trees
and a cool lemonade
ease the heat of a bright summer day.

The sand is not planned
to be part of a meal
even though there's a sandwich to eat.

But the sand is just grand
as a castle or boat
at the shore where the land and sea meet.

The sun is not fun
on a hot afternoon
when it shines on the treeless town square.

But the sun is the one
thing that everyone wants
for the week of the county-wide fair.

The rain is a pain
when it comes on the day
of a family picnic at noon.

But the rain is a gain
for the orchards and crops
that will need to be harvested soon.

In fall, when geese call,
and the leaves tumble down,
then the hard work of raking begins.

But the fall is a ball
when the leaves are heaped high,
for the kids jumping in. See their grins.

The day turns to gray
much too early, it seems;
time for sleeping—the curtains are drawn.

But the day on its way
turns the darkness to gold,
shouts, "The morning is here. Look, it's dawn!"

A hill in the chill
of the cold morning mist
won't call anyone out from inside.

But a hill is a thrill
when it's layered with white,
bringing people outdoors for a slide.

The ice isn't nice
when it covers the streets,
causing big feet and little to slip.

But the ice sure adds spice
for the last one in line
who skates fast at the end of the whip.

A drip that's a blip
from a leak in the roof
is a sound no one's happy to hear.

But a drip from the tip
of an icicle sings out
the welcome news springtime is near.

A worm, like a germ,
doesn't have many fans—
not for beauty or friendship or speed.

But a worm makes the firm
hardened earth into soil
for a garden that's ready to seed.